This book is dedicated to my Grandma Hattie.
Grandma always made
the best homemade ice cream.
We love you and miss you every day.

This book is also dedicated to the memory of my
best friend,
Joe "DJ BOOM" Young 2/9/2021

Book Design by Uzuri Designs
www.uzuridesignsbooks.com
bookdesigner@uzuridesignsbooks.com

Grandma Hattie's Ice Cream

by Jowan Smith

Grandma Hattie gave Aubrey 1 scoop of Cherry Ice Cream.

Cherry Ice Cream is
RED

Grandma Hattie gave Aubrey 2 scoops of Lemon Ice Cream.

Lemon Ice Cream is
YELLOW

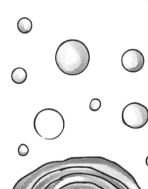

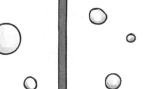

Grandma Hattie gave Aubrey
3 scoops of
Orange Ice Cream.

The orange ice cream is
ORANGE

4 Grandma Hattie gave Aubrey scoops of Cotton Candy Ice Cream.

Cotton Candy Ice Cream is
PINK

Grandma Hattie gave Aubrey 5 scoops of Mint Chocolate Chip Ice Cream.

Mint Chocolate Chip Ice Cream is GREEN

Grandma Hattie gave Aubrey 6 scoops of Blueberry Ice Cream.

Blueberry Ice Cream is

BLUE

Chocolate Ice Cream is **BROWN**

Grandma Hattie gave Aubrey 8 scoops of Grape Ice Cream.

Grape Ice Cream is

PURPLE

Grandma Hattie gave Aubrey
9 scoops of Vanilla Ice Cream.

Vanilla Ice Cream is
WHITE

10 Grandma Hattie gave Aubrey scoops of Black Licorice Ice Cream.

Black Licorice
Ice Cream is
BLACK

Grandma Hattie makes the best ice cream EVER!!!!

THE END

1 sandwich bag

1 Gallon Ziploc bag

1 tablespoon of sugar

½ cup of milk or ½ cup of half & half cream

¼ teaspoon of vanilla

2 tablespoons of table salt

- With the sandwich baggie put the sugar, milk and vanilla. Zip closed.
- Take the gallon sized bag and place the rock salt in bag and fill with ice cubes about 3/4 full.
- Place sealed sandwich baggie in with the ice and salt.
- Ziploc gallon bag closed.
- Give the bag to the kids to shake and roll filled bag over and over until frozen (about 15-20min.)

Yummy! Open and eat!

Com
Klarence
Coleman
235 - 238

CPSIA information can be obtained
at www.ICGtesting.com
Printed in the USA
BVHW092335150522
637012BV00002B/3